ARLO, MISS PYTHIA
and the
FORBIDDEN BOX

ALICE HEMMING
Illustrated by MIKE GARTON

My name is **ARLO** and:

1. I like to make notes to help me keep track of what is going on. And there has been a <u>lot</u> going on.

ME

Last year we were in 4X. Our teachers kept running away but then we got a new teacher, Mrs Ogg. She dressed in animal skins, carried a gnarled stick and took us on a school trip to a zoo full of real-life dinosaurs. We learned a lot about ourselves.

2. I struggle with saying long words out loud, especially if other people are listening. But then I did manage to say — <u>micropachycephalasaurus</u> in front of the whole class, so maybe I'm getting better.

3. I am now in class 5P. We are two weeks into the new school year with our new teacher, Miss Pythia. She doesn't wear animal skins but she is not like a normal teacher. I don't think so, anyway.

4. My two best friends are Nathan and Daisy-May. Daisy-May is really good at art and she loves animals. Nathan doesn't say much but he's very interesting if you really get to know him.

Other interesting people in my class are:
Paige: who is bossy but you get used to her.
AJ: you can't miss AJ. He is very LOUD.
Mitchell: throws things, breaks things, takes things without asking.
Olly and Molly: the twins who climb on anything.
Ronnie: one of the quieter ones. I sometimes forget he's there.

'Have you noticed anything pe-pecu-weird about Miss Pythia?' I asked.

There definitely *was* something weird about our new teacher. I just wanted to know if Nathan and Daisy-May had noticed too. It was Monday morning and we were in the playground waiting for Miss Pythia to call us into class. Daisy-May dangled upside down on the rollover bar and Nathan perched next to her.

'No,' said Daisy-May, turning a somersault. 'Anyone know what's on the lunch menu today?'

'Don't change the subject,' I said. 'I've noted

down some of the strange things about her.'

Daisy-May sighed and shook her head from her upside down position. Nathan sighed and shook his head the right way up.

'Like what?' asked Daisy-May.

Nathan didn't say anything; he never said much.

I opened my notebook and read aloud.

She always seems to know <u>exactly</u> what's about to happen.

'Like when she grabbed that pai-paint-paintbrush from Mitchell yesterday.'

We had been painting pots in red and black and Miss Pythia reached out to stop Mitchell's paintbrush going in Talisha's ear. It was millimetres away. Miss Pythia hadn't even looked in Mitchell's direction.

But Daisy-May was not convinced.

'*Anyone* would guess Mitchell would do

something he shouldn't with a paintbrush. Like put it in his pocket by "accident". Or stick it in Talisha's ear. It wouldn't take a genius to figure that out.'

Nathan nodded his agreement. I was not put off. I had loads more things on my list.

The symbol on the back of her neck.

It was like two capital Es joined back-to-back with a small circle in the middle. 'I sometimes feel like it's an eye, watching me. Do you ever get that?'

'Nope. And loads of people have tattoos,' said Daisy-May, spinning around again. 'My mum and my brother have about a gazillion between them. Even Casey K is thinking of getting one.'

Nathan nodded. Casey K was Daisy-May's biggest sister. Daisy-May had lots of big brothers and sisters. But I wasn't giving up.

'It's not just the tattoo. Even her name is pe-pecu-strange.'

I flicked to the right page in my notebook. I had looked it up online and copied it down.

'Look, it says right here.'

Pythia: The Ancient Greek high priestess at the temple of Apollo. One of the most powerful women in the ancient world, she served as the Delphic Oracle, where she prophesised future events.

'I don't know what that means,' said Daisy-May.

'She could predit-predict things – see into the future,' I said.

'So what? She shares her name with some Ancient Greek priestess,' said Daisy-May. 'My surname is Bacon and I'm a vegetarian. It means nothing.'

'What about her clothes? You have to admit they're a bit different. She wears that same white dress every day. And that snakey bracelet thingy round her arm.'

'So? She has her own unique style. And she likes snakes. I thought we'd established that. Anything else?'

I looked at my notes.

'No.'

Daisy-May returned to an upright position.

'For once, we have a nice, normal teacher, who likes us just the way we are. She doesn't shout, she isn't mean and she doesn't give us too much homework. I know Mrs Ogg was different. Mrs Ogg was special. But Mrs Ogg was a one-off.'

I had to agree with Daisy-May on this point. Mrs Ogg was our last teacher. Mrs Ogg was definitely one of a kind.

'We'll never replace her,' said Daisy-May, 'but Miss Pythia is lovely. Not different. Not Mrs Ogg. We need to accept that from now on, school life will be calm and boring, just the way it should be.'

Nathan nodded his agreement from his seat on the rollover bar.

'Will you stop agreeing with Daisy-May?' I snapped. Nathan looked at his shoes and I instantly felt bad. Sometimes I took it out on Nathan when I was really cross with Daisy-May. He never answered back.

'Sorry,' I mumbled.

Nathan smiled a small smile and Daisy-May jumped to her feet.

'Come on guys, don't fight. I can see Miss P about to open the door.' We headed for the 5P classroom and the door swung open. Clouds of sickly sweet-smelling smoke ballooned into the playground, revealing our teacher, dressed in a floor-length white dress with a lightweight purple scarf draped across her shoulders. In her arms she carried one of our class pets – a black and brown snake called Oleander – who was currently curled around her forearm and inching towards her left elbow. She laughed a high, tinkling laugh and beckoned us towards her with her right hand.

'Come, come, the children of 5P,
Bring your little minds to me,
The door is open; step right in,
A new adventure will begin.'

We walked through the doorway and hung our coats on the pegs, the same as always. Calm and boring, just the way school life should be.

We sat in our usual seats. The mood was calm. It was always calm in Miss Pythia's classroom. Oleander was back in his tank, spiralled in the corner. Laurel, the inquisitive ginger kitten, was curled up on the windowsill, looking out into the playground. Miss Pythia perched on her favourite high three-legged stool, and called the register. Everyone was here apart from Tony Abbes. He was never here.

'Lunch choices next,' said Miss Pythia. 'Starting with... Olly.'

'Red, please,' said Olly and Molly, the twins, together.

'GREEN PLEASE,' said AJ. We covered our ears. AJ was always so loud.

'What are the choices, again?' asked Mitchell, even though they were written on the board directly behind Miss Pythia. She didn't seem to mind.

'Green choice is pizza and red choice is battered fish,' she said.

'I choose pizza. Obviously,' said Mitchell.

But then Miss Pythia raised her hands and swayed her shoulders rhythmically from side to side. Her pupils grew wide.

'The truck will get stuck and we know what that means. The pizza's replaced with a jacket and beans.'

'Eh?' said Mitchell.

Miss Pythia shook her head rapidly and resumed her normal voice.

'Pizza, was it Mitchell? Lovely. Now who's next?'

I was next. I trusted Miss Pythia and opted for the fish. She seemed to think that pizza would be off today and I was not going to risk the school jacket potatoes. Had no one else realised that Miss P's predictions always seemed to come true? And even though she spoke in strange rhymes it sounded as though pizza would be off the menu at lunchtime.

Miss Pythia clasped her hands together in front of her and smiled.

'Before we start our new topic, Ms Weebly will be arriving with a special announcement. In fact, she will be here just about *now*.'

At the exact moment that Miss Pythia said the word 'now', Ms Weebly swept into the room. Our school Head. It was as if a lion had just walked in. We all sat bolt upright in our seats, on guard, in case she suddenly pounced.

Miss Pythia retreated gracefully to the back of the room and Ms Weebly took control. She looked about as pleased as she ever did to see our class, which was not at all. First, she glanced towards the snake tank.

'Is the beast locked away?' she asked Miss Pythia. Miss Pythia nodded, an amused expression on her face.

Then, with pursed lips and without a 'good morning', Ms Weebly launched straight into what she had come to say.

'Who here has ever been to the theatre?'

I put up my hand. I went to the Purple Hill pantomime with my family every year. I looked around the classroom. A few hands were raised. I put my hand down again. I didn't want to have to say the word pantomime out loud. My long words sometimes came out muddled. Anyway, Paige had already started speaking without being chosen.

'We go to the theatre in London once a month. I like to see musicals. Daddy says…'

But we didn't find out what Paige's daddy said. Ms Weebly shot her such a look that she put her hand down and trailed off, cheeks pink. Ms Weebly looked for somebody suitable to answer her question. She chose Mitchell.

'Mitchell, can you tell us about your trip to the theatre?'

'I went to see the new one about those ninja mice on a speeding train.'

There were murmurs of approval from the rest of the class.

'Ninja mice? I am not familiar with that play,' drawled Ms Weebly.

'It was awesome. The trailers were funny as well. There was this one mouse–'

Ms Weebly threw up her hands. 'That is the cinema! I am not talking about a *movie* theatre. I am *talking* about real theatre. Drama! Comedy! Shakespeare! Treading the boards! Real people and real actors.'

She tutted and gestured at us all to put our hands down.

'I am *talking* about "Play in a Day". This is a unique chance for Year 5 pupils, while Year 6 are away on their residential trip to the Isle of Wight. There will be an inter-school theatre showcase at St Cyrils's in two weeks' time. Three schools have been invited. Including St Cyril's. You will have to write the play, direct the play and perform the play. All in one day and all in front of an actual live audience.'

There were whoops of excitement. My heart lifted in my chest like a balloon. This was the sort of opportunity we had been waiting for. In 5P we had loads of skills that would make us perfect for a play.

I began to scribble in my notebook.

PLAY IN A DAY

<u>Paige</u>: a natural leading lady.
<u>AJ</u>: great voice projection.
<u>Naima</u>: amazing singing voice.
<u>Daisy-May</u>: always drawing – set design?
<u>Nathan</u>: something behind the scenes.
A playwright? Special effects?
<u>Olly and Molly</u>: daredevils – stunts!

For a moment, I dared to let myself dream. Maybe, just maybe, there was a role for me in all of this. I discovered when we went to the dinosaur zoo that I was good at organising things. I could be the director! I wouldn't have to stand up on stage and battle with long words. Maybe I would even have my own chair with ARLO printed on the back.

Ms Weebly's voice broke into my dream.

'Here, I have a leaflet about it for you to take home to your parents.' She produced a stack of leaflets from the folder she was carrying. She licked her thumb and forefinger to help separate the stack and handed the leaflets around the classroom. When she handed me mine, I was very careful not to touch the area that she had been holding. Ms Weebly's spit. Yuck.

'This year, we are lucky enough to be joined on the day itself by the one and only Jacques P. Lancaster.' Ms Weebly's eyes glazed over a little. Everyone else looked blank. Ms Weebly looked frustrated. She obviously expected us to know who he was.

'Jacques P. Lancaster?' she said again, 'The very famous film director! He directed the *Day of the Dinosaur* trilogy?'

I gasped. I love the *Day of the Dinosaur* films! I watch them all on my birthday *every* year, without fail. And we were going to see the director in real life.

Ms Weebly continued. 'Jacques P. Lancaster doesn't normally appear at school plays but he is a personal friend of the St Cyril's Head. Jacques P. Lancaster will be there. All your families will be there. The school governors will be there. Prizes will be given for best actor, best set design, that sort of thing. Get this right, and it will be glory for Purple Hill Primary...' Her eyes narrowed. 'Get this wrong, it will mean utter humiliation for all concerned, especially me. And I will not... be... happy.'

I gulped.

'To get it right, you will have to work as a team. And I really hope you *do* get it right although, given your track record, I find that highly unlikely,' she said, forcing her mouth into a smile which was more of a grimace.

We would have to work as a team. My heart, which had been floating like a balloon, popped on Ms Weebly's spiky words and sank.

Currently, Paige and AJ were fighting over

the last leaflet, Daisy-May was doodling on Ronnie's English book, and Mitchell was leaning backwards in his chair to loosen the lids of all the water bottles stacked behind him. Our class was smaller than average (lots of children hadn't come back after the summer) and although we had many strengths, working as a team was not one of them. The big question was, could we learn to work together in just two weeks?

Ms Weebly had finished. She left as abruptly as she'd arrived; she probably didn't want to stay in the classroom with us (and Oleander the snake) longer than she had to. Miss Pythia closed the door gently behind Ms Weebly and smiled.

'It sounds as if we are going to have a lot of work over the next couple of weeks. Some of us have never been to the theatre before. Maybe we should find out what it's all about.'

A wave of excitement ran through the room.

A lot of work, yes, but not Maths or English or Science. This sounded like fun work.

Miss Pythia rummaged under her desk.

'Let me find my theatre file.' She disappeared from view and began removing items and placing them on the desk. A box of ballpoint pens. A teddy bear. A dictionary. And another, very interesting looking item.

'That's it,' she said, 'I've found it.'

But the eyes of 5P were not directed towards the theatre file. We were all looking at the last item she removed. A box. A bright, beautiful box the size of a shoe box but with a claw-like foot at each corner. The golden metal of the box reflected a shaft of autumn sunlight. I shielded my eyes to look at it.

It was as if Miss Pythia had brought out a big box of chocolates; we left our chairs and moved instinctively towards it. We crowded around the desk, eyes fixed on the intricate floral engravings adorning the lid and the sides. On the

top was a familiar symbol. Like a sun, or an eye. Like the eye pattern on the back of Miss Pythia's neck.

'What's in the box, Miss Pythia?' asked Naima.

'I am afraid I can't tell you that. This box doesn't belong to me, you see. I am keeping it safe for someone else.'

Everyone spoke at once.

'Can I see the box, Miss Pythia?'

'May I touch the box?'

'CAN I SMELL THE BOX?'

'Yes, you may touch the box. You may rub the box. You may even smell the box.'

She let each of us run a finger over the embossed patterns. I touched the sun-like symbol on the lid. It was warm.

Miss Pythia wrapped her arms possessively around the box and moved it to the side of the desk.

'Although you may touch this box, whatever

you do, you may not open the box. Opening the box is strictly forbidden.' Her expression darkened. 'Opening the box would have dire consequences. Dire consequences. Do you understand? *Dire consequences.*'

It was unlike Miss Pythia to lay down strict rules. That must mean she was serious. We all nodded. Yes, we understood. Miss Pythia whipped her purple scarf around in front of her. She was swaying again. She closed her eyes and hummed a few notes then began to speak.

'Leave the box alone, I say, but
one of you won't manage that.
And we all know what people say,
That curiosity killed the cat.'

Miss Pythia shook her head as she said, 'Now, where did I put that theatre file…' But I was no longer thinking about the theatre. I guessed that all sixteen of us were thinking the same thing.

Just what, exactly, was in that box?

The rest of the morning went slowly. In Science, we had to put stuff in jugs of water until it all spilled over the sides. Apparently some old guy had discovered this happened when he was in the bath. I wasn't that interested; I just watched the clock until lunchtime when I could talk to my friends.

At lunchtime, pizza was off the menu. The delivery truck had got stuck. The fish was still on but the green choice was now jacket potato.

I remembered Miss Pythia's cryptic warning from earlier:

'The truck will get stuck and we know

what that means. The pizza's replaced with a jacket and beans.'

'Miss P was right! I am so glad I listened to her advice,' I said, slicing through the crispy batter of my fish.

'I like school jacket potato and beans, especially the burnt bits,' said Daisy-May, tucking in.

Nathan looked sadly at his plate; I knew he would have preferred pizza.

'So what do you reckon is in the box, everyone?' asked Daisy-May, looking round the table. The three of us were sitting on one side, with Paige, Georgia and Ronnie on the other.

This was interesting. I turned to a fresh page in my notebook and wrote,

WHAT'S IN THE BOX?

'My theory is that she's keeping mice in there to feed the snake,' said Daisy-May.

I wrote it down.

'Euchh,' said Paige, turning pale. 'I hope not. I think it's treasure! Sparkling gemstones and coins…'

'And valuable jewellery!' added Georgia. They squealed.

I wrote that down too even though it wasn't particularly original.

'What do you think, Nathan?' asked Daisy-May.

Nathan made some square shapes with his hands – one way and then the other.

'Fish?' guessed Daisy-May.

'Dance music?' tried Paige.

But I knew what he meant.

'Boxes?'

Nathan nodded.

'Little boxes inside the big box?' Interesting idea.

'But what's inside the little boxes, Nathan?' asked Daisy-May.

Nathan giggled. His giggle set us all off laughing, even though I didn't quite know why.

'Go on, Nathan, tell us what's inside,' I said, knowing he would speak when he was relaxed and laughing.

'Nothing!' squeaked Nathan, and we all fell about laughing again. All apart from Ronnie. He wasn't laughing or saying much. Just chewing, thoughtfully.

'Aren't you interested in what's in the box, Ronnie?' I asked.

'Nope,' he said. 'I saw the look on Miss P's face when she warned us not to touch it. I think whatever is in there is *bad*.'

'Bad? Like what?' I asked.

'Like a curse,' said Ronnie, through a mouthful of beans. 'Or worse. Whatever it is, I don't want to know. I reckon we should keep that box firmly shut.'

Silence fell. Shouts and clinking cutlery echoed around the canteen but no one on our table spoke a word.

I carefully added 'curse or worse' to the bottom of my list and then clicked the lid firmly on my pen.

Daisy-May turned around her lunch tray with gusto.

'Arctic roll!' she announced. 'My favourite.

I'm not going to let this get warm.'

This time I was grateful for Daisy-May's change of subject. We tucked into our puddings happily and no one mentioned the box again.

After outside play we came back into the classroom to find Mitchell already there. He was standing by Miss Pythia's desk, his hand resting on top of the golden box.

'What are you doing, Mitchell?' I asked.

'Just having a look. Miss Pythia said it was ok if we just look at it.'

Ronnie's words echoed in my head:

'Curse or worse, curse or worse.'

And Miss Pythia's words:

'Curiosity killed the cat.'

I edged next to Mitchell and placed my hand next to his on top of the box. I knew what he could be like and I didn't want this box opened, even accidentally. Mitchell wandered back to his seat and I moved to follow him but walked straight into Miss Pythia. She swayed and bent closer to my height. Then she whispered, too quietly for the others to hear,

'They want it open - why, oh why?
Someone needs to keep an eye,
You were the hero at the zoo,
And once again, it must be you.'

I nodded my understanding but then she shook her head and looked at me as though she'd just walked in.

'Take a seat please, Arlo,' she said. It was as if she had no memory of what she said in her funny trances. But, whether she remembered or not, Miss Pythia was right. I had to keep an eye on 5P. I was responsible. I was not going to let that box out of my sight.

'I hope you enjoyed your lunches, despite the issue with the delivery van,' said Miss Pythia. There was a sleepy feeling in the classroom. Oleander the snake was having an after lunch snooze and Laurel was curled up in Miss Pythia's lap. I always felt like curling up myself after lunch.

'I know how sleepy you are feeling, so I thought I would wake us all up with an interactive lesson on the theatre, to get us in the mood for *Play in a Day*. I always think the best way to understand something is to go right back to the beginning. Can anyone here tell me where and when the theatre began?'

I had no idea but loads of hands shot up. Some of my classmates just liked putting their hands up, even when they had no idea of the answer.

'WAS IT HERE IN PURPLE HILL?'

'No, AJ, it all began much further away.'

'The West End?' guessed Paige.

'No. Good guess, but theatre in the UK began in the sixteenth century. The true origins of theatre were in another country long before that. I am going to take you back to where it all began…'

Miss Pythia pulled down the blind and asked Georgia to turn out the light. Then, she swiped her hand across the interactive whiteboard screen. A photograph appeared showing a semi-circle of old-looking white stone seats rising up to meet a deep blue sky.

'This is Greece. Ancient Greece. About two and a half thousand years ago.'

'This doesn't look like the theatre where we go. The theatre where we go has red curtains and comfortable seats,' said Paige.

'It has taken a long time for theatres and plays as we know them to develop but this is what they looked like when they began. That stage area at the bottom is called the *orchestra*. The seating area could hold lots of people, up to 15,000. Shall we take a closer look?'

We nodded. Miss Pythia lit a scented candle on the teacher's desk and the room began to fill with perfumed smoke.

'Fire risk,' muttered Ronnie, but I got the feeling that Miss Pythia wasn't too bothered about Health and Safety breaches. She seemed to do what she fancied, like bring a kitten and a snake into the classroom.

I coughed and waved a hand in front of my face.

'I can't even see your face, let alone the whiteboard,' I whispered to Nathan. He giggled and waved his hands as well.

Gradually, the smoke began to clear. And along with the smoke, our desks and the classroom seemed to vanish all together. It was as if we were in the theatre itself, looking down at the stage area. The theatre no longer looked ancient and crumbling; it looked as if it had been built yesterday. The stone seats were even and bright white, in striking contrast with the deep blue sky – nearly as deep a blue as our school jumpers – and the green hills behind. This was Ancient Greece but as it was then, not as it appeared in the books. We were sitting right near the top of the theatre, surrounded by empty seats. We looked down into a paved, semi-circular area, with a stage and a temple-like building behind.

Figures in clothes a bit like Miss Pythia's were putting on some sort of performance on the stage.

'Where are we, Miss Pythia?' asked Paige in

a high voice.

'We have come to Ancient Greece to learn a little more about the theatre,' said Miss Pythia.

'But it's like we are at-act-actually here,' I said.

'The mind is a powerful thing,' said Miss Pythia.

We looked at one another. Was this really just a clever trick? It felt real enough to me.

Mitchell and some of his friends climbed down a few steps to get closer to the show.

'Why is no one else watching the play?' asked Paige.

'They are rehearsing,' said Miss Pythia.

'Why do their faces look so creepy?' asked Ronnie.

'They are wearing clay masks to show how they are feeling. They also have special shoes and padded outfits so we can see them from all the way up here.'

Ronnie looked away. 'I don't think I like masks,' he said.

The masks were bigger than a normal person's face and they weren't lifelike but had holes for eyes and mouths. Two of the actors wore masks with turned-down mouths. The other had a circular mouth that looked surprised. That one was also wearing a beard.

'This is a tragedy so they are wearing sad faces. In a comedy, they might have happy faces and silly features with big noses, that sort of thing. Wearing masks also allowed the men to play different characters. One man might play a queen, a hunter and a servant all in the same play.'

'Are they all men then?' asked Daisy-May.

'Yes, in those days they were all men or boys. Women didn't start acting until much, much later. Not until about 1660 in England.'

'What is the play about?' asked Georgia.

We stared down at the stage. The actor with the beard had his hands over his eyes and was staggering around in a circle.

'This is the story of Oedipus Tyrannus, a tragic king. This is near the end – the part where he has blinded himself.'

AJ put his hands to his own eyes and staggered dramatically.

'I CAN ACT TOO. AARGH, MY EYES, MY EYES,' he said.

Everyone laughed and copied him, clutching at their faces and shouting dramatically and scattering in all directions. It was pretty noisy. The actors below noticed us and began pointing. One of them shouted something. They left the semi-circular orchestra and started to climb the steps at the bottom of the seating area.

'Time to go!' called Miss Pythia. Half of us began running in one direction and half of us in the other. It was never easy to round up 5P. But eventually we were all seated back at the top near Miss Pythia, who whipped her purple scarf around us in a circular motion. I watched the scarf and the sky until it was all a whirling pattern of blue and purple. The seats and the stage were a blur of white. I blinked in the bright sunlight and put my hand over my eyes. It took me a while to realise that it was autumn sunlight streaming through the 5P window, not onto the ancient theatre.

I looked around at my classmates. Many of them were shielding their eyes and blinking just like I had been.

Miss Pythia flicked the lights back on in the classroom and we were back where we started, at our desks. The noise level in the classroom rose as we all asked our friends the same question: had we really just been sitting out in the sunshine on the steps of an Ancient Greek theatre?

'That was weird, wasn't it?' I said to Daisy-May, next to me.

'It was very realistic,' she said.

'But it was like we were actually there!' I looked at my arms, which had turned slightly pink in the baking hot sunshine.

'That's the whole point of interactive whiteboards,' said Daisy-May. 'They do make you feel as if you're actually there.' I wasn't convinced. I had never seen anything like that happen on an interactive whiteboard. Most of our other teachers had to ask the Year 6's in to help them work them.

And this wasn't like Daisy-May. She was normally the first person to believe the impossible. She had managed to single-handedly ride a woolly mammoth all the way home from the dinosaur zoo after all.

'Why are you being like this?' I asked.

Daisy-May sighed.

'I miss Blanket,' she said. Blanket was the woolly mammoth. When Mrs Ogg left, he was taken to a zoo on the other side of town. It wasn't very far away but difficult for us to get there by ourselves.

'But what's Blanket got to do with Miss Pythia?' I asked.

Daisy-May raised her eyes to mine.

'I don't want Miss Pythia to leave and take her pets with her. I want a nice normal teacher. One who is going to stay.'

Now I understood. Oleander and Laurel. It was always about the animals with Daisy-May. I didn't know what to say but luckily Miss Pythia interrupted the moment. She took a yo-yo from Chloe's desk and held it up.

'Look, children. A yo-yo!' she said. I thought she was about to confiscate it but she simply said, 'This toy was also popular with children in Ancient Greece!'

The noise level returned to normal as we watched Miss Pythia's yo-yo skills, then she smiled and asked us to draw what we had just experienced at the theatre. Daisy-May put her head down and started drawing a face like one of the ones we'd seen on the masks. Creepy, but good as always.

We continued the rest of the lesson in silence, concentrating with our heads down towards the desks. The rest of the hour went quickly and before I knew it, Miss Pythia clapped her hands together.

'Playtime!' she announced. 'Don't forget your raincoats.'

'Raincoats?' asked Paige. 'It's bright

sunshine out there!'

We all filed out of the classroom, past Miss Pythia's desk and the golden box. The trip to the theatre had distracted the others and they had forgotten about the box but I hadn't. I ran my hand lightly over it as I walked past. I grabbed my waterproof from my peg and watched the rest of the class run out into the sunshine in just their polo shirts and jumpers. A grey cloud seemed to come out of nowhere and move in our direction.

When would the rest of 5P cotton on to the fact that Miss Pythia's predictions were always spot on?

At home, I spent a lot of time looking up facts about Jacques P. Lancaster.

FACTS ABOUT JACQUES P. LANCASTER

* He started directing short films when he was just a little bit older than me.

* His Day of the Dinosaur Trilogy was the fastest selling dinosaur trilogy of <u>all time.</u>

* He owns - 117 - pairs of designer sunglasses.

50

* He hardly ever signs autographs – he's just too busy. His autographs sell for hundreds of pounds online.

I wondered if I might get Jacques P. Lancaster's autograph at *Play in a Day*. I wouldn't sell it. I would treasure it forever.

At school, we were working hard for *Play in a Day*. We were allowed to prepare certain things in advance, although we had to make all the props and costumes and do all the rehearsals on the day itself.

'We can agree on which story and write our script,' said Miss Pythia. 'The theme is "Myths and Fairytales".'

'Ooh, how about Goldilocks?' said Paige, flicking back her long, blonde hair.

'No,' we all shouted together.

'Little Red Riding Hood?' said Olly.

'Yeah – I'll be the Wolf,' said Mitchell, opening his mouth wide and snapping his hands together. He looked more like a crocodile than a wolf to me.

Paige screamed, then AJ joined in, leaning over his desk towards her and miming wielding an axe.

'I WANT TO BE THE WOODCUTTER. I'M GOING TO CHOP OFF YOUR HEAD – CHOP CHOP.'

Miss Pythia smiled and calmly closed her eyes to the chaos. She looked as though she was lying on a beach, not standing in front of sixteen thunderous nine-year-olds. Strangely, her lack of reaction seemed to quieten everything down and the noise ebbed slowly away.

'Not fairy tales,' said Daisy-May, after a moment's silence. 'Can we do something like we saw in the theatre? With the masks?'

Miss Pythia opened her eyes and a smile spread across her face.

'Good idea, child. We must write our own play but we could base it on an Ancient Greek myth.'

Nathan put up his hand.

'Yes, Nathan?'

Miss Pythia's eyes met Nathan's. They gazed at each other for a moment. 'Good idea, Nathan. We could base our play on the story of Pandora's box.'

Nathan had not said anything. But somehow Miss Pythia had understood what he wanted. I wrote this down in my book.

Possible telepathic abilities?

Nathan beamed and nodded enthusiastically. How did he know about Ancient Greek myths? Although... Nathan did know loads of stuff that other people didn't know. Probably because he didn't speak much. He listened more.

But the rest of us didn't know the story of Pandora's Box. We fired questions at Miss Pythia.

'Is it a comedy or a tragedy?' asked Daisy-May.

'I would say it was a tragic tale, wouldn't you agree, Nathan?'

Nathan nodded.

AJ stood up and waved his hand.

'DOES IT HAVE A LOAD OF BLOOD IN IT?'

'No blood, AJ, but there is much misery and suffering.'

'COOL!'

'Who was Pandora?' asked Chloe.

Miss Pythia smiled. 'Pandora was the first woman on earth.'

'I thought that was Eve?'

'Not for the Ancient Greeks. They believed something different. Let me show you.'

Miss Pythia dimmed the lights and placed her palm on the interactive whiteboard. Was she about to whisk us back to Ancient Greece again? I braced myself. But this time she switched on the visualiser on her desk and the screen turned plain white. She took a striped tin from the shelf behind her desk, opened it and began to remove simple black paper cut-outs. She placed these on the visualiser like shadow puppets to make a scene. There were little people: two men and a bigger, god-like figure with a beard and a thunderbolt. She began to tell the story.

'Once, long ago, human beings lived in happiness and harmony with the gods. But it was not to last because of the actions of two brothers, Prometheus and Epimetheus. Prometheus offended Zeus, king of the gods, by stealing fire from Mount Olympus. Offending the Ancient Greek gods was never a good idea. Zeus had a clever plan to punish Prometheus.'

It was strange, the paper cut-outs were just basic shapes on a white background but Miss Pythia had us hooked. Maybe it had something to do with her soothing voice. Her words floated around the room.

'The gods made a woman – a beautiful woman – and sent her to Earth. Her name was Pandora. Prometheus warned Epimetheus not to trust the gods but Epimetheus didn't listen. He married Pandora and they were happy. Maybe they would have stayed that way, but the gods had not finished with their meddling. The gods would have their revenge, no matter what.'

That sounded ominous.

'Zeus sent a box to the couple as a wedding present. Not a large box but an important looking box. A box of the gods, no less. He asked Epithemeus to guard it, telling him that he needed to place it in the care of someone he trusted. Epithemeus took his duty seriously. How hard could it be not to open a box? But Pandora was curious. "What could be inside?" Pandora wondered to herself, "What can possibly be in a box that belongs to the gods? Fine robes? Perfume? Treasures?"'

'Snake food?' whispered Daisy-May.

'Little boxes?' I offered. Daisy-May laughed at this. It would have normally set Nathan off giggling but he was staring intently ahead, towards Miss Pythia's desk.

'Pandora was told to stay away. "Keep away, my dear. No good can come of going near the box. Just keep well away," said Epithemeus.'

This story was starting to sound familiar.

'But Pandora couldn't stop thinking about the box. She felt it calling to her... Open the box, open the box.'

I had stopped looking at the cut-out box on the whiteboard at this point. I was looking at a different box – the one on Miss Pythia's desk. And someone else was looking too. Nathan.

'Open the box, open the box…' repeated Miss Pythia. Next to me, Nathan's eyes were fixed firmly on the box.

'Are you ok?' I whispered, but Nathan didn't seem to hear me. His eyes were glazed. For a second, I thought he was going to get up and walk towards the box. Was *this* box calling to *him*?

'Stay in your seat please, Nathan,' said Miss Pythia, kindly but firmly, and Nathan blinked rapidly. The strange look vanished from his eyes and Miss Pythia continued with the story.

'One day, Epimetheus was sleeping. Pandora just couldn't help herself. She took her chance and tiptoed towards the box. "I will just have a little peek," she said to herself, "then I will make sure everything is back just the way I

found it. No one will ever know..." '

I sank down in my seat. Don't open the box, Pandora! But Miss Pythia continued.

'Pandora checked again to see if Epithemeus was still sleeping. He was. So she took her opportunity. She stood on tiptoes and reached the box on its high shelf. Pandora edged the box off the shelf and into her open hands. It felt surprisingly light. She ran her fingers lightly over the decorations on the lid. Then, ever so slowly, she unclasped the lid and opened the box...'

Miss Pythia paused. I held my breath. It was going to be bad, I knew it.

'To Pandora's horror, there was not a treasure in sight. Instead, out flew all the problems of the world. Sadness, sickness, hate, and envy. All released forever.'

With one sharp movement, Miss Pythia flung the shadow puppets into a scattered heap, making sudden crazy patterns on the screen. I

shielded my face with my hands. I half-expected
the world's evils to actually fly towards me.
Daisy-May laughed. Miss Pythia continued.

'Pandora raced here and there, desperately
trying to catch the troubles and put them back
into the box. But her efforts were in vain. She
could not catch a thing. They flew out and away
from her, ready to cause misery. Human beings,
who had lived in peace and prosperity, now
faced famine and sickness. They experienced
jealousy, anger and hate. Pandora

had released suffering and there was no turning back.

The gods' punishment was complete. Humans had brought this upon themselves. All through one person's curiosity.'

Miss Pythia switched off the projector and the screen went grey.

AJ looked stunned for once. 'THAT IS HARSH,' he said.

I leaned forward in my seat. 'Was that the end of the story? What happened to Pandora?'

Miss Pythia wandered between our desks so that everyone in the front row had to twist around in their seats to follow her.

'No, no, children,' she said, softly. 'This was not the end of the tale. You see, even in the darkest hour, you can always find a tiny glimmer of light.'

Miss Pythia crouched down towards the floor and stood up again with arms stretched out in front of her and hands cupped together. What was she holding?

'Was there something else in the box?' asked Daisy-May.

'Yes, child, yes, there was. *When Epithemeus awoke to find the havoc that she had unleashed, Pandora begged to be allowed to open the box just one last time. Epimetheus agreed. After all, what harm could it possibly do now?*'

Miss Pythia gazed around the room.

I sat up straighter. Miss Pythia slowly opened her hands like a book. A single white butterfly flew free. We watched as it fluttered erratically towards the ceiling, the sunlight catching its wings.

'*At the bottom of the box, was hope,*' she said, opening a window so that the butterfly could escape into the sunshine. '*Pandora may have released suffering into the world but she also*

introduced us to hope. And when there is hunger,
disease or poverty, hope will always be there for
us, like a light in the darkness.'

We watched the butterfly dance in the empty
playground before it vanished from sight.

'So, what do you think, 5P? Shall we use
Pandora's Box as the basis for our play? A story
of suspense, violence and sadness? The
beginnings of all human pain and suffering?'

There was a moment's silence and then,

'Yes!' we all chorused.

6

'I want to be Pandora,' said Paige.

'I want to be Pandora,' said Talisha.

'I WANT TO BE PANDORA,' said AJ.

Everyone squealed with laughter.

'What, it was all male actors when we watched that play in the theatre,' said Olly.

'Luckily, we now live in more enlightened times,' said Miss Pythia. 'We will choose the best person for each role. Whether they are a boy or a girl.'

'Miss Pythia, how are we going to decide who does what?' asked Paige.

Miss Pythia smiled.

'Have you ever heard of democracy?'

I had. 'Isn't that where you vote on stuff?'

'Yes. This is a concept that also began in Ancient Greece. It comes from the Greek words *Demos* meaning people and *Kratos* meaning power. So democracy is when the people have power.'

It seemed like everything had begun in Ancient Greece. I wasn't sure that democracy would work for 5P. I had hoped that Miss Pythia would decide rather than my classmates. I was not sure that I trusted 5P to decide anything.

Miss Pythia wrote all the roles on the board. The idea was that if people thought they would be right for the role then they would nominate themselves. Then, if there was more than one candidate, the class would vote. I had my eye firmly on the director role. I wasn't going to put up my hand for anything else.

'We will start with the role of Pandora,' said Miss Pythia. 'I know that a few of you are interested in playing this role. Please put up your hand if you would like to play Pandora.'

Paige, Talisha and AJ all put up their hands. Then, to my surprise, Nathan also raised his hand. I nudged him to put it down. Nathan couldn't play one of the main parts. He didn't even speak most of the time.

'Why don't you help write the play?' I whispered. He would be good at that. He shook his head and stuck his hand up higher.

'Now we vote,' said Miss Pythia. 'We will

vote with a show of hands. Remember, you can only vote for one person. I'll give you all a minute to think about it.'

Talisha didn't get many votes. She wasn't quite as popular with the other girls as Paige. Lots of the boys voted for AJ. I thought he would make a disastrous Pandora. Far too loud. He would ruin the play. I was torn. Nathan was one of my best friends, but I didn't honestly think he'd be able to play the role of Pandora. He was too shy. I'd never seen him act before. And if I didn't vote for Paige, AJ might win.

I made my decision and voted for Paige. She might be annoying sometimes but she had quite a loud voice and was a bit of a drama queen. Nathan looked at me with wide, disappointed eyes. He got just one vote – from Daisy-May.

It was decided. Paige had five votes, AJ four, Talisha two and Nathan one.

Paige smiled smugly. 'I am now Paige of the Stage,' she said.

Talisha scowled. 'Let's put Paige in a cage,' she said.

AJ said, 'OH WELL'.

Nathan buried his face in his hands. I patted him gently on the back but he didn't look up.

'You'd be good at scriptwriting – why don't you nominate yourself as a writer?' I repeated, but he didn't look up and shook his head from his face-down-on-the-desk position. I felt a bit bad but Nathan would be giggling again soon – he always got over stuff like that quickly.

Next, we had to choose Epimetheus – Pandora's husband.

'I vote for Arlo,' said Paige. My face grew red. She had liked me since I saved her from the Apatasaurus at the Dinosaur Zoo. But I shook my head.

'Er, no,' I said. 'I don't want to act. Anyway I can't say Epi-Epith-Epim–that guy's name.'

In the end, we voted for Yusuf.

'HAHA YUSUF IS PAIGE'S HUSBAND!

YUSUF LOVES PAIGE. YUSUF WANTS TO
KISS PAI–'

Yusuf put the wastepaper bin over AJ's head
and he went remarkably quiet. Nathan would
find that funny. I nudged him with my elbow
and smiled, but he didn't respond.

'Are you going to be in the play, Miss P?'
asked Mitchell.

'No. You will be responsible for every part of
this play. I will be able to relax!' She laughed
her high, tinkling laugh.

'What about Oleander and Laurel?' said
Daisy-May.

Miss Pythia laughed again.

'You can't mean you want them to appear on
stage?' she said.

'Why not?' said Daisy-May. 'They are part of
this class too. And they would add atmosphere.
St Cyril's had a real donkey for their nativity.'

We had all heard about the donkey at St
Cyril's. They had even made it into the local

paper. Ms Weebly had a cutting of the news
article on the wall of her office.

Daisy-May fixed her pleading eyes on Miss
Pythia.

'I'd look after them,' she said. 'Pleeeeease?'

'Very well,' said Miss Pythia. 'You may be
the animal trainer. But you must look after them
well. Any signs that they are scared and they go
straight back in their crates.'

Daisy-May nodded. She would be good at
this.

We voted for all the rest of the acting roles
and the backstage jobs too. I wrote the whole list
down in my notebook, just in case.

PLAY IN A DAY ROLES

Pandora — Paige
Epimetheus — Yusuf
Narrator — AJ

Prometheus – Mitchell (also fake blood and screams)
Zeus, King of the Gods – Chloe
Chorus – Naima, Georgia, Tony Abbes (if he turns up)
Stunt people – Olly and Molly
Lighting/special effects – Jack and Sofia
Curtain – Nathan
Animal training/scenery/props – Daisy-May

Only three people now didn't have jobs – me, Talisha and Ronnie.

'We still need a director,' announced Miss Pythia.

'What does the director do?' asked Molly.

'The director has the overview of the play. They pull everything together,' said Miss Pythia.

'Like Jacques P. Lancaster,' I said.

'Sounds boring,' said Talisha.

'But aren't they sort of like the boss?' asked Chloe.

'Sort of,' said Miss Pythia. 'They need to be able to lead. We need someone with the right skills. Someone who notices what is going on.'

I patted my notebook. I always noticed what was going on. But had anyone noticed me noticing?

'Someone who can keep calm in a crisis,' continued Miss Pythia.

I had kept calm at the dinosaur zoo when Mitchell was nearly eaten by a T-Rex. But did anyone remember that?

I raised my hand.

'Are you nominating yourself?' asked Miss Pythia. I nodded.

Daisy-May immediately shot up her hand.

'I vote for Arlo,' she said. Thank you, Daisy-May. Yusuf and Jack turned around in their seats to stare at me. They hadn't been at the dinosaur zoo so they hadn't seen me saving the day.

'I vote for Talisha,' said Georgia.

The class voted. Nathan voted for Talisha. He

must have still been cross about the Pandora
thing. I was sure he'd get over it quickly. He
must see that he couldn't act in this play. And it
didn't matter in the end. I won by three votes.
I was going to be the director.

Talisha was not impressed.

'So what am I going to do?' she asked.

'You have a wonderful singing voice,' said
Miss Pythia. 'You can be in the chorus with
Naima and Georgia if you like.'

Talisha muttered and shot me daggers with
her eyes. She was going to make my life a
misery because of this. But I didn't care – I was
so pleased with my new role.

'And there is always an assistant director. Are
you happy to perform that role?' Miss Pythia
asked Ronnie. He nodded happily.

I guess there was always an assistant director,
and it did give Ronnie a job to do, but I was the
actual director. And the director was (sort of) the
boss of the play.

I turned to a fresh page in my notebook and drew the director's chair with my name on the back.

My dream was becoming a reality.

7.

Before we knew it, *Play in a Day* arrived!

We had written the play, we all knew our roles and we were ready to make the costumes, rehearse and perform. Everyone piled onto the coach, ready to go to St Cyril's. The driver was big and hairy. He wore what looked like a white sheet draped around him and one shoulder was bare. I thought I recognised him but couldn't think from where. Miss Pythia walked the length of the coach,

checking that everyone was buckled in. She wore Oleander draped across her shoulders like a scarf.

'Where's Laurel?' asked Daisy-May. She took her responsibility as kitten trainer very seriously.

'Oh, silly me, I forgot to put her in her travel basket. Could you fetch her for me? Choose a friend to go with you.'

'Sure,' said Daisy-May, unclipping her seatbelt and getting out of her seat. 'Come on Arlo,' she said. Nathan sat near the front because he got travel-sick. Part of me was glad that I didn't have to sit next to him with him not talking to me. He didn't talk most of the time, of course, but his latest not talking to me felt different. He was actually ignoring me ever since I voted for Paige. Not that it was personal – I was only thinking of what was best for the play. And he'd be much better at operating the curtain than acting. He'd realise that soon.

Daisy-May and I headed back to the classroom. Daisy-May found the pet carrier in the corner and began throwing cat treats into it in an effort to coax Laurel inside. As she held the door open and spoke to Laurel in a low, soothing voice, I stood by Miss Pythia's desk.

My hand rested lightly on the forbidden, golden box. My fingers tingled. It would have been very easy to unclip the lid and have a peek inside but I wasn't going to do that. I was the one who Miss Pythia trusted to look after it. But what if one of the other children got their hands on it when we were away? Someone from another year group? Or even a teacher? Ms Weebly wasn't joining us at St Cyril's until the performance later. What if she opened the box? I couldn't risk leaving it here.

There was only one thing for it. I was going to have to take it with me. I picked the box up with both hands. It felt warm, like it had the other day, and lighter than I expected.

'What are you doing?'

Daisy-May's voice behind me made me jump. I'm not sure why – it's not like I was doing anything wrong exactly. She had persuaded Laurel into her travel basket and gripped the pet carrier with both hands, all ready to go.

'Nothing,' I said. 'I just don't want the wrong people getting their hands on the box, that's all.'

Laurel mewed from inside the carrier.

'I don't know why you're so interested in the box,' said Daisy-May.

'I'm just keeping it safe,' I said.

I wrapped my waterproof tightly around the box – the last thing I wanted was for it to open up accidentally – and tucked it into my backpack. It stuck out at the top and I couldn't do up the zip, but it would have to do. As we rejoined the others on the coach, I held my backpack close to me, with both arms wrapped around it. I didn't want anyone seeing that I'd brought it with me; they would ask too many questions.

When we got back to the coach, Mitchell and Chloe had nabbed our seats at the back so we sat near the front. The coach set off straight away. Mitchell had somehow got hold of Paige's bag, which was covered in fluffy pompom keyrings of every colour, including one in orange that was nearly as big as the bag itself. It was impossible *not* to play with Paige's bag.

'Can I just have a play with this big orange pompom?' asked Mitchell.

'No! Give it back!' shouted Paige. Mitchell threw the bag to AJ, who threw it to Talisha. Talisha threw it to Molly, who took pity on Paige and threw it back from a distance but missed, and hit the window behind her.

'Oops,' said Molly.

'Oh no, you've broken my mirror!' said Paige, removing the cracked pocket mirror from the side pocket of her bag and examining the fractured glass.

Talisha laughed. 'Even Pandora should be able to go for a few hours at St Cyril's without checking how beautiful she looks,' she said.

Ronnie sat bolt upright in his seat.

'It's a bad omen. Seven years' bad luck for a broken mirror,' he said.

Paige's hands flew to her cheeks.

'Oh no! Is it really? Bad luck for me or for everyone? Miss Pythia, will I really get seven years' bad luck?'

Miss Pythia glided towards the back of the bus as she counted heads, remaining perfectly balanced as the driver swung around the windy roads to St Cyril's.

She took the plastic-framed mirror from Paige.

'No, child, a broken mirror is not bad luck. That is just a silly superstition. When I look in this cracked mirror I see your faces reflected

back at me countless times. So much hope. So much possibility.'

Miss Pythia waved the mirror around her so we all saw our reflections. She handed the mirror back to Paige with her usual smile. Paige relaxed.

'I've got loads more at home,' she said.

The coach pulled to an abrupt stop at some traffic lights and Miss Pythia gripped the back of my seat. Her face changed; the smile dropping away. She froze, rigid, gazing out of the coach window, eyebrows drawn together and eyes fixed on the sky.

'What is it?' asked Ronnie.

'The mirror may not be a bad omen but these birds above us are not a good sign.'

'What, the pigeons?' said Daisy-May.

Miss Pythia shook her head.

'These are not pigeons, child, but something more sinister, I fear.'

Miss Pythia began to sway.

'When crooked-taloned birds fly west.
Then all may not be for the best.'

Ronnie's eyes widened. I gulped. We needed good luck for today, not a bad omen. Nobody said a word but we exchanged glances. Even Nathan looked over and met my gaze for a split second. I wished he was sitting next to me.

The coach started again and Miss Pythia resumed her normal calm appearance. She stopped staring at the sky and made her way back up to the front of the coach. I looked at Daisy-May.

'O…K…' said Daisy-May.

Then Mitchell poked his head out into the aisle.

'I was just wondering… will there be popcorn today?'

'That's the cinema, Mitchell,' said Daisy-May.

*

We turned onto the drive that led to St

Cyril's, where the *Play in a Day* was taking place. St Cyril's was very different to our school. Our school was at the bottom of a big hill called Purple Hill, even though it was grey. St Cyril's was at the top of a slope, dotted with trees. I stared out of the window. A light breeze scattered the orange leaves like petals. The school itself was built from grey bricks with arched windows. It looked more like a church or a museum than an actual school. A buzz went around the coach.

'Miss Pythia, do you think that we'll win any prizes today, or will all the others be better than us?' asked Georgia.

Miss Pythia appeared to consider the question for a moment before she swayed from side to side and replied.

'The waxing moon glows soft and pale
And so St Cyril's might prevail
But if you focus on the play

Then this might be your lucky day.'

'Well, that's cleared that up, then,' said Georgia.

Jacques P. Lancaster greeted us all in St
Cyril's school hall. *The* Jacques P. Lancaster. He
was wearing sunglasses – it was his signature
look. He stood at the front, like an assembly,
with slides on the screen behind him. He told us
a few facts about himself and talked about what
it was like directing films with multi-million
pound budgets. I took detailed notes. A smiling
photograph of him clutching a *Best Director*
award beamed out from behind him. Would
there be a Best Director award today? Would the
awards be little golden statues like the one
Jacques was holding? And… would I win? One

thing was certain – I was going to try my very hardest. He then told us his top five tips for directors. I scribbled it all down in my notebook. This was valuable information.

After his talk, Jacques invited questions. I had lots of questions but I didn't dare put my hand up in case I said something wrong. AJ asked one.

'WHAT DOES THE "P" IN YOUR NAME STAND FOR?'

'Harharhar,' laughed Jacques deeply. 'What do you think it stands for?'

'PAUL? PATRICK? PAIGE? PRIMROSE? PYTHIA? PHYLLIS?'

Some of the children from other schools, who weren't used to AJ, giggled.

Jacques interrupted, 'I get asked that question a lot but I have never given away

the answer yet. Maybe one day–'

'–PABLO? PENFOLD? POTIPHAR? PONTIAS? PACEY? PARWINDER? PROSPERO? PLUT–'

'ENOUGH!' shouted Jacques. AJ stopped. Jacques ran his hand through his messy black hair and breathed deeply.

'That is enough questions for this morning,' said Jacques. He collapsed into a chair and the St Cyril's Head stepped in to explain how the day was organised. We would all split off into different classrooms depending on whether we were rehearsing or carrying out behind the scenes roles. Directors and assistant directors were allowed to float between the rooms to get an idea of the bigger picture.

We filed out of the hall.

'That was really interesting, wasn't it?' said Ronnie. I kind of nodded to show that I'd heard him, but I was busy consulting my notes from Jacques' talk.

ROLE OF THE DIRECTOR

(1) There are two types of director:
Those who give the actors and crew freedom,
for example, to come up with their own
dialogue.

(2) Those who control every part of the
production, and insist that the actors and
crew follow their instructions precisely.

I decided I was a Type 2 director. The type
who would control everyone.

Different activities were taking place in
different classrooms at St Cyril's. They had
rooms for subjects here, like art and science,
whereas we did everything in the one classroom.
It was hectic. Someone had to check up on all
the teams to make sure that the teams were all
working towards the same vision. And that
someone was me. I was going to keep complete
control so that my play would be perfect. I

walked towards the art room with my notebook. Ronnie followed along behind.

'What shall I do?' he asked. Of course, he was the assistant director.

DIRECTOR'S TOP TIP #1
Everyone works best on a full stomach.

'Have you got any crisps?' I asked. Next to Daisy-May, Ronnie always had the best packed lunches.

'Crisps?' he asked. 'Um, yes, but the packed lunches are in the dining room.'

'Would you mind getting them? I work much better on a full stomach.'

'Sure, ok.'

Ronnie disappeared and I opened the door to the art room. Props and Scenery. It smelled of paint. They would need to have their orders from me early on to give them time to get everything ready for this afternoon. A sheet was suspended from the ceiling. The plan was to paint directly onto sheets and hang them at the back of the stage. I saw Daisy-May's elbow poking out from behind it. She had obviously started already.

'We need the backdrops to look Greek. Olive trees, blues sky, white temples,' I said. I had a vision.

'Like this?' asked Daisy-May. She pulled me round to her side of the sheet, which was already virtually covered in paint. Blue sky, white buildings, olive trees.

'Wow,' I said. 'You worked quickly.'

'Yeah, I skipped the director talk. What else do we need?' she asked.

I looked at the list in my notebook. 'We need masks, like those ones we saw in Ancient Greece. Mainly sad ones, as it's a tragedy. One each for Paige and Mitchell and AJ.'

'I made a start on those already,' said Daisy-May. She pushed a box under my nose, which was full of assorted masks. I took one out. It wasn't made of clay, like the ones in Ancient Greece. Instead, it was drawn on cardboard, with eye- and mouth-holes cut out and elastic at the back to hold it on. It had the same creepy feel as the original. This particular one had a large round mouth hole. I realised that I was pulling the same expression in response to this huge pile of masks.

'Anything else?'

'I need a name for the back of my chair and a megaphone. And a di-ditec—a director's badge.'

'What do you need those for?' asked Daisy-

May, looking me right in the eye.

'For ri-di-shouting stuff out.'

She wrote 'director' on a sticky label and Arlo on a piece of white paper. Then rolled up a piece of silver card into a cone shape, stuck it together with sticky tape and snipped off the end. She handed it all to me.

Ronnie appeared behind me with a bag of crisps. I took it and ripped it open. I was starving.

Ronnie took the megaphone and spoke through it. 'Do I need one of these as well?' he asked.

'No. You can share mine if you need to,' I said, taking it back. I doubted he would be shouting out any orders.

'Need anything else?' asked Daisy-May, smiling.

I checked my list, munching the crisps.

'No, I think that's everything.'

'So we don't need any more props?' asked

Ronnie, grinning along with her.

I shook my head. What were they giggling about?

'No more props at all for Pandora's *Box*?' said Daisy-May.

'No I don't think so… Oh! The Box! Of course. Just testing!'

'Shall I make that then?'

I nodded.

Daisy-May showed me a shoe box.

'I thought I could spray this gold and cover it with some plastic jewels?'

'Erm, yes. Very good.'

I turned to leave but Daisy-May thrust the bag of masks towards me.

'Here you go,' she said. 'Don't forget to give these to the actors.'

I handed the bag of masks and the empty crisp packet to Ronnie.

'Do I have to carry the masks?' he asked. 'They're creepy.'

'I've got my hands full with my notebook and megaphone, I'm afraid,' I said, as Ronnie carried the bag at arm's length.

I felt satisfied so far. Now that props and scenery knew what to do, I could go and organise everyone else.

DIRECTOR'S TOP TIP #2

Sometimes people have to do things they don't want to do – it's up to you to explain why.

'There is no way I am wearing *that*,' said Paige, looking at the mask as if it were an old nappy.

'But it's a Greek trad-trag–a Greek play. You saw them at the Greek theatre. They were all wearing masks!'

'How are the audience supposed to know

what I am feeling if they can't see my face?'

'They know what you're feeling from the es-ep-expression on the mask. Look – happy! Sad!' I held the masks in front of me.

Talisha was clutching her stomach, laughing. 'I don't mind one. Give it here, I'll be Pandora.'

Paige stomped over and swiped the mask from Talisha's grip.

'Fine, I'll wear it,' she said.

'I'm just trying to make my play as auth-authen–as real as possible,' I said through my megaphone.

'Your play, Arlo? Your play? I am Pandora – the main character – I think you'll find it's *my* play!' snapped Paige.

'The play's not called Pandora – it's called Pandora's *Box* and Daisy-May's making that,' argued Talisha. 'It's actually more her play. And what about Ronnie? He's assistant director so he's doing half the work.' Ronnie shrugged but looked quite pleased.

'I'M THE NARRATOR AND I HAVE THE MOST WORDS SO IT'S MY PLAY.'

'No way,' said Mitchell. 'Miss Pythia told us the story. It is *her* play – obviously.'

'Come on ev-everyone, it doesn't matter who's play it is,' I said. *We all know it's mine,* I thought. I tried to change the subject. I pulled out a chair and stuck my director's sign on the back.

'How is the rehearsing going?' I shouted through the megaphone.

'Does that cardboard cone actually make your voice any louder?' asked Talisha.

'Yes. It's my megaphone. It makes my voice clearer.'

'NO IT DOESN'T,' said AJ.

'How is the play coming along, anyway?' I shouted again.

Paige put her hands on her hips.

'Talisha keeps standing in front of me and no one's going to be able to see me behind her big head. Can't you make the chorus stand over there?'

'Good idea,' I said. 'Chorus, can you stand over there on the left, please.'

'We can't stand there – it's too close to AJ and *his* big head blocks the audience's view of us.'

'Ok – maybe if you all stand on the right.'

Talisha rolled her eyes.

'*That's* no good. That's where the box is going to go and we have to be able to see the box.'

I looked around. Nathan, Olly and Molly didn't seem to be doing anything.

'What are you three doing?' I asked.

'Nathan, you're the…' I checked my notebook. 'Of course, you're doing the curtain. You need to open it before the play begins and close it when it ends.'

Nathan narrowed his eyes.

'Maybe today, while everyone's rehearsing, you could practise a bit? So that… you know, you can do it smoothly?'

Nathan didn't respond. He carried on watching the actors and mouthing the lines silently to himself. Well, good. That would help him to remember the right times to work the curtain. I turned my attention to the twins.

'What are you doing?'

'We're the stunt people,' said Olly and Molly,

together.

'Do we need any stunt people?'

'Yes. I'm an evil spirit. When Paige opens the box, I'm going to swing down on a rope,' said Molly.

'No, I am,' said Olly. 'I'm a better swinger. You need to hold the rope.'

'No way, that's the boring bit. Don't you think I'd be better at swinging, Arlo?' asked Molly.

'And where shall we stand?' asked Talisha.

They all stood silently in front of me, waiting for the next instruction. I felt a bit hot and flustered. Directing was more tiring than I'd thought. Maybe I wasn't a Type 2 director. Maybe I was a Type 1 director and I was going to give these guys their artistic freedom. I lifted the megaphone to my mouth.

'You are going to have to sort this out between yourselves,' I shouted.

'What?' cried Paige, 'I can't sort anything out

with Talisha – she's ruining my play.'

'It's not your play.'

'IT'S MY PLAY…'

I jumped up from my seat and left them arguing in the hall. They all had good points but there was no getting away from the fact that I was a very important person in the play. Sort of the boss. The play wouldn't happen if it wasn't for me. If it was anyone's play it was mine. I straightened my director's badge and went to see what was happening in the special effects department. Ronnie came too.

'Arlo, I was just thinking, we could stand AJ on a block behind the chorus so that the audience can see him–'

'–Sorry Ronnie, can you be quiet for a minute please? I'm just checking my notebook to see who's next on the list.'

'Oh, ok,' said Ronnie, his face pink. He went very quiet but I could still feel him standing there as I checked my notebook. His presence was starting to get on my nerves.

Suddenly, Miss Pythia was standing there with him. Had she been walking behind me since the hall? She leaned towards me and said, gravely,

'Arlo, you can't do it all,
Pride always comes before a fall.'

I nodded politely. Right now, I didn't have time to think about Miss Pythia's strange rhymes. I needed to organise the special effects team.

The hours flew by and, before we knew it, it was time to perform. Purple Hill were the last ones in the line-up, after St Cyril's and Red Hill Primary. We had already watched their plays in rehearsals and they were really good. St Cyril's performed 'Rapunzel'. There were no real life animals in this one but they had amazing lighting that made the stage look like a forest and a cardboard tower that looked real. Red Hill had focused on the music in their production of 'Little Red Riding Hood' and their singing and dancing was all perfectly choreographed. And now it was our turn. I sat in the wings with

Ronnie and Nathan. Nathan still didn't look very pleased about being the curtain guy and he still didn't appear to be talking to me, even though we were sitting right next to each other in a tiny space. What would Jacques P. Lancaster do?

DIRECTOR'S TOP TIP #3
Make sure everyone knows they are a valuable member of the team

I punched Nathan lightly on the arm.

'We couldn't do this play without you, buddy,' I said, in a director-ish way. 'The curtain guy is a valuable member of the team.'

Nathan raised his eyebrows and did not reply. Oh well, I'd tried.

Ronnie was looking over my shoulder into my notebook. I snapped it shut. Ronnie shuffled his feet, twiddled with the end of the curtain pull and sighed.

'What do we do while the play's going on – direct from back here?' he asked me.

'Kind of. I'm prompting. I keep my eye on the script and if anyone forgets their lines, I read them out to remind them.'

Lots of people had forgotten their lines in rehearsals. Not at St Cyril's or Red Hill. Only 5P. I suddenly felt sick and my palms were sweaty. I rubbed them up and down my trouser legs to dry them and stared at the script.

'Can I prompt too?' asked Ronnie.

I was beginning to wish that there'd been an extra part in the play for Ronnie.

'Not really. Prompting is more of a one-person job. Why don't you… just keep your eye on things and let me know if you spot anything out of the ordinary.'

'Ok,' said Ronnie. He took off his glasses, gave them a wipe, then replaced them and stared at the stage, unblinking.

The St Cyril's school hall was packed. I could see my mum. Daisy-May's family were all there, including her grown-up brothers and sisters. They took up nearly an entire row. Ms Weebly was sitting near the front. She put on her sunglasses and wrapped a headscarf around her. Anyone would think she didn't want to be recognised. Jacques P. Lancaster had his own chair, like a throne, at the back of the hall.

Daisy-May appeared next to me, with Laurel in her pet carrier. She was going to release her onto the stage when Paige made her entrance. Laurel was our secret weapon. With a cute, fluffy kitten on stage, maybe nobody would notice the forgotten lines. My mouth was dry. I swallowed.

'Are you ok?' asked Daisy-May.

'I'm a bit n-nerv—I mean—there are lots of people here. And they are looking at us,' I said.

'That does normally happen with plays,' said Daisy-May. 'Try breathing deeply. I'm going to go and get Oleander.' Daisy-May was going to give Oleander to Talisha after Pandora's Box was opened, to provide a bit of atmosphere.

There was just a minute to go. The curtain was pulled across and I checked that everyone was in their correct places.

Chloe, as Zeus, was standing on a box in the middle. She wore a wise mask and a long beard. Yusuf and Mitchell were just below her, ready to go.

AJ was standing just to the left of the stage and the chorus were next to him, although Talisha was still jostling to get nearer to centre stage. Olly and Molly were high up above the stage on a wooden structure, holding on to a rope and pulley system.

'GOOD LUCK EVERYONE!' said AJ.

'No, no, no!' Ronnie shouted back. 'You have to say "Break a Leg!"'

I glared at him.

'It's bad luck otherwise,' he said.

DIRECTOR'S TOP TIP #4

When you're ready, you're ready. Know when it's time to take a step back and let the actors get on with it.

We were as ready as we would ever be.

The St Cyril's Head announced our play. Nathan pulled the cord to squeakily draw back the stage curtains and the 5P *Play in a Day* began. It was not the great start I had hoped for. At first, nobody said a thing. AJ, the narrator, was supposed to be the first to speak but for once he seemed lost for words. He had his script in front of him so he didn't need a prompt. I coughed gently. Nothing. I took off my shoe and threw it at him. It hit AJ on the shoulder and seemed to spur him into action.

'MANY YEARS AGO, GODS AND MEN LIVED IN HARMONY,' he began. AJ's voice certainly made the audience sit up and listen. The actors on stage performed the first scene as we'd rehearsed. It all went pretty well. Paige was a great Pandora. Even if you couldn't see her face behind the mask, her dancing skills came in handy. Even when she walked, she remembered to point her toes. She looked like a true Ancient Greek heroine. I was glad we hadn't ended up with AJ in the role.

Yusuf remembered all his words, and the chorus sounded beautiful. They sang a real Greek song that Miss Pythia had taught us. The audience was transfixed, and so was I. I kept my eye on the script. I didn't want to lose my place. So far things were going pretty well.

Daisy-May had released Laurel onto the stage with Paige but now she pulled my arm and whispered urgently, 'Arlo, what am I going to do? Oleander's gone missing! I promised Miss Pythia that I'd look after him.'

'Shhh, keep your voice down. We have to be quiet back here.'

I had one eye on the twins, who seemed to be fighting about something in their spot above Paige's head. Right now, a missing class pet was the least of my worries.

'We'll put a poster up or something

afterwards. What kind of snake is he?'

'A python,' said Daisy-May.

She suddenly had my attention.

'A python? But aren't they poi-poin-poisonous?' I whispered.

'No,' said Daisy-May.

I relaxed and went back to keeping one eye on the script and another on the stage.

Daisy-May turned to walk away and as she went I thought I heard her say,

'They squeeze their victims to death.'

I tried not to think too much about missing
animals. Right now, my play was going just the
way it should and that was all I cared about.

'THE PULL OF THE GOLDEN BOX WAS
TOO MUCH FOR PANDORA TO RESIST,'
said AJ. I followed along in my script. Word
perfect.

'Wow, Daisy-May did such a great job
making that box,' said Ronnie, speaking a little
louder than he should.

'Shhhh,' I said, trying not to lose my place.

Pandora danced closer to the box. Ronnie
tugged at my sleeve.

'Don't you think it looks exactly the same as Miss Pythia's?' he asked.

What did he mean? I was getting a bit fed up with all the distractions and I shrugged him off but I did still stare out from behind the curtain to check.

The box that Paige was dancing towards was a bright, beautiful box the size of a shoe box but with a claw-like foot at each corner. It was the box from my bag. The box from the classroom. The box that we were absolutely and completely forbidden to open and the box that was my responsibility to keep shut. And I knew exactly which part of the play was coming next – Pandora was about to open the box.

My heart raced as I looked towards my rucksack, in the corner behind the curtain. My waterproof had been removed and a box was poking out of the top.

A box made not out of shiny gold metal but out of spray-painted gold card. The box that

Daisy-May made. It took my brain a little while to compute. Someone had switched them!

Stunned, I peered out into the audience and caught Miss Pythia's eye. Her hands were raised and she was slowly shaking her head. I forgot about keeping quiet. For a moment, I forgot all about my play. I frantically leapt out from my position behind the curtain and flapped my arms to distract Paige.

'No, no, don't open the box!' I shouted.

'NO, NO, DON'T OPEN THE BOX,' shouted AJ. He must have thought I was prompting him.

'Don't open the box,' repeated the chorus, swaying from side to side.

'Don't open the box,' said the St Cyril's kids in the front row. What did they think this was, a pantomime?

Paige looked briefly towards me and then continued with her dance. The light levels dropped in the hall as the sky outside darkened to a deep grey. Was it a storm? It had been such a lovely day earlier. The hall grew dark and the only light came from the box itself, which glowed a bright gold. Paige's surprised mask – its mouth an open O – was bathed in a warm yellow light. She moved closer to the box and bent to lift the lid. Sheet lightning flashed outside, lighting up the high windows in the school hall. On stage, the grotesque masks of the chorus appeared white in the gloom. My heart raced faster.

The chorus continued to sing, 'Don't open the box, don't open the box, don't open the box,' in a low whisper, as if they were in a trance.

What was in the box? Ronnie's voice echoed in my mind, *'curse or worse, curse or worse'* and Miss Pythia's words, *'curiosity killed the cat.'*

What was happening? Should I rugby tackle Paige and stop her opening the box? But I was too slow to act.

'PANDORA COULD NO LONGER RESIST THE TEMPTATION,' read AJ.

Paige lifted the lid.

The chorus wailed.

I craned to see but I was too far away. Was that a pair of eyes glinting? I gulped. Clouds of dark smoke poured from the box. Strange shapes formed that looked like wispy ghosts or spirits. The smoke filled the stage and poured into the audience.

'Is that dry ice? Quite remarkable,' said the St Cyril's Head from the front row. It was especially remarkable because, as far as I knew, the special effects team hadn't used any dry ice.

AJ kept reading.

'OUT OF THE BOX FLEW ALL THE PROBLEMS OF THE WORLD. DISEASE, MISERY AND POVERTY WERE UNLEASHED.'

I turned to Daisy-May.

'Why did you put Miss Pythia's box on stage?'

'What do you mean? I don't care about the stupid box. I just want to find Oleander.'

'Well if you didn't put it there, who did?'

'I don't know? Talisha? She was annoyed with Paige for getting the part and you for being director. Mitchell? Just to see what would happen? It could be anyone, Arlo, but it wasn't me.'

AJ continued to read his narration. Thick smoke poured from the box.

'HUMANS BEGAN TO SUFFER.'

That was the twins' cue to swing down from the rafters but Olly and Molly were still fighting over whose job it was to hold the rope.

Meanwhile, Mitchell came onto the stage with a tube of fake blood. He was supposed to squeeze it gently but, in his excitement, he squeezed too hard and the tube went flying out of his hands, spraying fake blood as it went. The tube landed on the stage, Yusuf took a step backwards and squashed it. Scarlet liquid spattered across the actors' white robes and covered everyone in the front row, including the St Cyril's Head. A small child in the audience wailed.

'It's not real!' I said, trying to reassure the

boy, but his mum was already whisking him to the back of the hall. As the smoke began to clear, the sound system blasted out 'Twinkle, Twinkle Little Star' at top volume and glittery snow began to drift down from above, even though we were supposed to be in baking hot Ancient Greece. The special effects were going all wrong.

Through the snowstorm, I spotted something very strange. There were five people on the

stage wearing masks. I counted in my head.
Yusuf had been wearing a mask. So had
Mitchell, Paige and Chloe. But that only made
four. Who was the fifth? Was there an evil spirit
from the box causing havoc on stage? Like a
curse... or worse?

Just as I tried to figure out who the extra
person was, Molly made her decision to leap
from the rafters. But Olly wasn't holding the
rope and Molly flew down more rapidly than

intended. The audience gasped as she skidded across the stage, narrowly missing Paige but kicking Talisha in the back of the legs. Talisha turned round to see Paige standing behind her.

'Hey!' she cried and pushed Paige. Paige lurched backwards and hit her head on the stage. Paige lay flat out on her back, not moving.

At the same time, Olly copied Molly and jumped down from the rafters. The rope he was clinging to unfurled at rapid speed, knocking a wooden beam as it went. Laurel the kitten ran onstage. At the same moment, the beam fell with a crash. Where was Laurel? I had lost sight of her in the crowd on stage. I ran to inspect the damage. Something was sticking out from under the beam. Something ginger and fluffy.

My heart fell into my socks. We had killed Laurel! *Curiosity killed the cat.* We had opened the box and poor, innocent Laurel had paid the price.

And then Nathan did the most sensible thing

that anyone had done since the start of this mess of a play. He wound in the curtain.

'Interval!' shrieked Ms Weebly from her place in the audience, then she left her seat and stormed towards us.

14.

Anger erupted from Ms Weebly like steam from a boiling kettle. And it was steaming mainly towards me.

'You're the director, aren't you? Well *direct*!'

It was all my fault. I was supposed to be the one with the vision and the leadership skills but I had failed. I was the world's worst director. I ripped the paper sign from my chair and threw it on the floor, with my name badge on top of it. I had absolutely no idea what to do. I looked at Miss Pythia, who was looking after Paige. Paige sat up and blinked steadily.

'What shall I do?' I mouthed to Miss Pythia.

'Think of Pandora,' she said.

Pandora was all I was thinking about! I raced through the story in my mind, picturing the shadow puppets. What had happened? Pandora released the evil spirits. Disease and suffering all round. Blah blah blah. Then what? Miss Pythia's voice played in my head.

Pandora's box reminds us that in our darkest hour, when we are close to giving up, there is always hope.

Hope. Of course. We would find hope still inside the box.

AJ didn't seem to notice that the curtains had been pulled across for the interval. He was still reading from the script.

'PANDORA THOUGHT SHE MIGHT AS WELL OPEN THE BOX ONE LAST TIME.'

'We're taking a quick break, AJ!' I called. 'I'm going to check what's in the box.'

I ran to the box and everyone ran with me, apart from Pandora herself, who didn't look as though she'd be running anywhere for a while. I was overtaken by the crowd. What could possibly be inside? More smoke? Fireworks? Everyone wanted to see. I needed hope and hope would be somewhere inside the box. It just had to be. But I couldn't get through the crowd to see for myself.

I peeked through a gap between Olly's and Molly's heads. Talisha opened the lid. There were gasps.

'What's inside?' I called.

'It's empty,' said Talisha.

Empty? It couldn't be. There had to be hope. There was always hope. Miss Pythia said so. Maybe they had missed something. I pushed between Olly and Molly to the front of the crowd.

'Let me see,' I said. I peered into the box, into every corner, searching. Talisha was right. It was absolutely empty. All I could see was the shiny bottom of the box and all of our faces reflected back at us. All the disappointed faces of 5P. Where was hope when we needed it?

Miss Pythia's voice played in my head once again. This time from the coach.

When I look in this mirror I see your faces reflected countless times. So much hope. So much possibility.

Then it clicked. All our faces reflected back at us. 5P were at the bottom of the box. We were the last hope.

DIRECTOR'S TOP TIP #5
Admit when you've made a mistake

'It's us!' I shouted through my megaphone. 'We are the last hope for this play. We can sort out this mess, but we need to work together.'

'I thought you said it was *your* play, Arlo!' said Talisha.

I lifted my megaphone again. The edge of the cardboard was getting soggy and crumpled where it had been near my mouth. The others were right; it didn't really make my voice any louder. I put down the cardboard cone and spoke in my usual voice. Everyone was near enough to hear. I looked around at the scowling faces.

'No! It isn't my play! I thought it was but I was wrong. It's not Paige's play either, or Yusuf's or AJ's. None of us can perform this play on our own. We need every single one of us working as a team, from the main star to the guy who gets the crisps.'

Ronnie was at my side immediately. I needed his help now. I needed everyone's help.

'What shall we do, Arlo?' asked Ronnie.

'First, we all need to lift that beam.'

Daisy-May wrapped her arms around the beam and pulled. 'It's too heavy,' she said. It was an impossible task for just one person but with all of 5P on the case it would be easy. Half of us stood at one end and half of us stood at the other. I got ready to give the signal. Then,

MIAOW!

A cat poked its head out from behind the

curtain. Not just any cat – Laurel! Daisy-May rushed to her and scooped her up. She was absolutely fine! But if Laurel was safe and well, then what was that ginger fluffy thing sticking out from under the beam?

'Let's lift the beam! 1-2-3!' I cried and we all heaved together. The thing under the beam wasn't a squashed cat, or a squashed anything. It sprang back into a fluffy spherical shape as soon as the weight was removed.

'My pompom!' cried Paige, stretching out an arm from where she lay on a folding chair backstage. Daisy-May threw her the oversized orange keyring. Paige sat up and removed the wet flannel from her brow for a moment. 'But how did my pompom get there?' she asked.

I knew who I would put my money on. We moved the beam safely out of the way and I turned and looked at Mitchell, who was wearing his most innocent expression. It didn't really matter who had taken it. Paige had her pompom back, we hadn't killed a kitten and now we could finish this play in style. Daisy-May cuddled Laurel, who looked confused to be receiving so much attention.

'I'm sorry for accusing you of swapping the boxes,' I said to Daisy-May. 'I think I know who it was now. Will you help make the rest of the play a success?'

'Of course,' said Daisy-May. 'What do you want me to do?'

'First, I need Nathan.'

'That's easy. He's right behind you.' She looked over my right shoulder.

I turned. Nathan stood there, a guilty expression on his face. I didn't have to ask – he had switched the boxes. I could tell. He knew I knew, as well. He had been drawn to that box all along. Maybe the great box swap was the only way he could get to see what was inside. But there wasn't time to talk about it now. Right now, we needed to all work together.

Paige was currently horizontal. I needed someone to step in. Someone who had been watching the actors and would know what to do.

'Nathan, can you help?' I asked. 'We need a new Pandora.'

16.

Nathan smiled. The first smile I'd seen from
him in a while.

He nodded.

'The play can go on! Is everyone in?' I
shouted, without my megaphone. I stretched out
my hand and Nathan put his on top of mine.
Daisy-May and Ronnie followed. Then, one-by-
one, fourteen hands slapped down on top of
mine.

'It's time to draw back that curtain once
again,' I said. 'I'm afraid Nathan's going to be
busy on stage. Ronnie, would you mind doing
the curtain?'

Ronnie gave a grin.

'No problem at all,' he said.

We stood in our new positions. Nathan wore Paige's Pandora mask. I did have to wrestle it out of Talisha's grasp but I explained that Talisha had a new role now – as the star of the show.

The second half of the play was much shorter than the first and so much more professional. This time we worked together. AJ read his lines beautifully and Nathan made a surprisingly convincing Pandora. He may not have been quite as light on his feet as Paige and he was a little shorter and wider. But he didn't have any words to say in this part and was in the right place at the right time every time. Nobody would have guessed that he hadn't rehearsed with the other actors.

When Nathan, as Pandora, opened the box for the second time, Talisha was Hope. Talisha danced onto the stage draped in white floaty fabric. As she twirled and waved her arms, it made me think of the butterfly back in the classroom. The audience broke into applause at that, before we'd even got to the end.

Then, for the grand finale, Naima and Georgia sang a song about hope. It had a familiar tune but made-up words. We all joined in. All of 5P together, singing and swaying together like a proper team.

'All you need is hope.
All you need is hope, hope.
Hope is all you neeeed.'

Miss Pythia swayed along to the music, chanting *'Hope, hope, hope.'*

Ms Weebly took off her dark glasses and unwound her headscarf. Maybe she wasn't going to disown us after all.

After the plays, there was a lot of clapping.

We clapped the other schools and they clapped us. We clapped our teachers. We clapped St Cyril's. The biggest clap was saved for the end – for Jacques P. Lancaster – who had come all this way just for *Play in a Day*. It was time for him to present the prizes. My earlier dream of a Best Director statue flashed into my mind but I quickly shook my head. No way was that going to happen.

Jacques P. Lancaster smiled a wide smile. 'Wow. I am really impressed. Three wonderful plays, put together in just one day.'

He did look properly impressed, not like he was just saying it. Then it was time for the prizes. He told us all the things that he had loved about the St Cyril's play. 'What a play! The costumes! The lighting! The painting!'

St Cyril's won the prize for 'Best Scenery and Special Effects'.

Clap, clap, clap. Cheers and whistles from St Cyril's.

Then Jacques P. Lancaster told us all the things that he had loved about Red Hill Primary's play. 'What a play! The music! The lyrics! The choreography!'

Red Hill Primary won the prize for 'Best Musical Score'.

Clap, clap, clap. Whoops from Red Hill.

My hands stung. I started to clap one palm on the back of the other hand just to make a change. But what about us? Surely Purple Hill had to win something? Nathan, sitting next to me, crossed his fingers and held them up. I did the same.

'Now, Purple Hill Primary,' said Jacques P. Lancaster. 'What a play! Do you know, I don't think I've ever seen anything quite like it. I was most impressed by the original take on the theme. A real Ancient Greek tragedy with lots of authentic touches. The acting and singing was something else but what really impressed me was the way you didn't let a couple of technical hitches bring you down. You all worked together to get through. That is why I am awarding you the prize for *Best Teamwork*!'

Purple Hill went wild. Miss Pythia tapped me gently on the shoulder.

'You should collect the prize, Arlo.'

Me? But I was the one who'd messed it all up. I looked around me. My classmates nodded but I shook my head.

'Let's all go up together. As a team.' We all stood up, giggling and nudging one another, and made our way to the front of the hall. I went first. My cheeks were hot. I was going to shake hands with the one and only Jacques P. Lancaster.

To Arlo
A great director and team leader
All the best.
Jacques P. Lancaster

Jacques P. Lancaster signed my notebook! I managed to ask him while the audience was clapping Purple Hill. The others went to sit back down and he said, 'Stay up here for a minute, kid.' He wrote me a special message. Then he had to go.

'Another awards ceremony,' he said, as if they got tiresome after a while. Then a car with windows darker than the lenses in Jacques' sunglasses screeched up outside the school. Jacques P. Lancaster jumped inside and, in seconds, was gone.

The rest of us hung around the hall while we waited for the coaches.

Daisy-May, Nathan and I sat in the now nearly empty front row. They admired the autograph and we chatted about the play.

'There's just one thing I don't understand,' I said. 'Who was that with you on stage after Paige opened the box the first time? In the happy mask?'

Nathan looked blank and shook his head.

'It couldn't have been anyone in 5P,' said Daisy-May. 'The person in the mask was tall. Taller than AJ, even.'

So who had it been? A child from another school? Or an actual evil spirit? Not for the first time, I wondered exactly what had been in that box.

We stopped talking for a second and stared around us, maybe all contemplating the same thing. Ms Weebly was at the other end of the front row, talking to the St Cyril's Head. She sounded like she was trying to impress him.

'Oh yes, I have quite a group of little thespians at Purple Hill. Theatre has always been very important to me–'

As she spoke, she reached around to the back of her chair, feeling for something along its width. Her scarf? But the scarf was pooled at her feet. She frowned and turned.

Daisy-May leapt out of her own chair and towards Ms Weebly.

'Oleander! I thought we'd lost you!' She lifted the snake from Ms Weebly's grasp before he had the misfortune to be worn as a scarf.

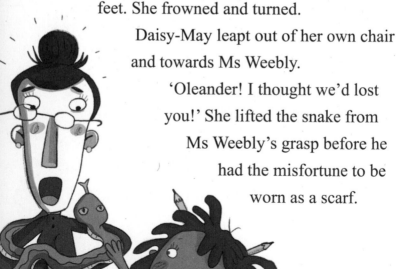

Ms Weebly screamed and pointed to the snake as we made a swift exit.

'Let's get Oleander back to Miss Pythia,' said Daisy-May as the St Cyril's head tried to calm Ms Weebly down.

'Where is Miss Pythia?' I asked. I hadn't seen her since she'd asked me to collect the award.

Mitchell walked over and pointed to the stage. 'She's up there,' he said.

Miss Pythia stood in the centre of the stage, her purple scarf wrapped tightly around her. She carried her three-legged stool in one hand and Laurel in a pet carrier in her other hand. The golden box was by her feet.

I sighed.

Miss Pythia looked ready to leave.

19.

All the children of 5P found our way back to the stage from different spots in the hall. We gathered around Miss Pythia, drawn to her like Pandora was drawn to the box. Miss Pythia's usual upturned mouth ran in a straight line.

'What a joy it has been to work with you all, children,' she said. 'A wonderful play. A wonderful team. A wonderful class. I will remember each and every one of you.'

'WHERE ARE YOU GOING?' asked AJ.

'I'm going home. I have been looking after this box for someone else and now it has been opened I must return it.'

'When will you be back?' asked Chloe.

'That is a question to which I just don't know the answer,' said Miss Pythia.

Daisy-May stepped forward and draped Oleander around Miss Pythia's shoulders, then poked her hand through the side of the pet carrier and stroked Laurel. Tears ran down Daisy-May's face. Miss Pythia placed the stool on the stage for a moment and patted Daisy-May's shoulder. She began to sway.

'It may be time to say goodbye,
But wipe the tears from your eye,
The golden box is open now,
And all of you have found out how,
To work together just as one.
We learned a lot and had some fun,
I taught you and you taught me.
But now 5P becomes 5B.'

Miss Pythia took a step back and whisked off her purple scarf. She held it by the end, at arm's length, and shook it firmly so that it moved in a snake-like pattern. I watched, mesmerized. We all watched. As I gazed at the purple blur, I heard a squeaking and I realised that someone was drawing the curtain quickly across the stage. It grew suddenly very dark. There was a **BANG!** from above and we all looked up. Glitter rained down like the fake snow from earlier. A familiar smoky sweet smell filled the stage.

When we looked back down, Miss Pythia, her pets, the stool and the golden box had all gone.

We all stayed sitting on the stage, staring into the middle. Nobody spoke for a while. Then the muttering started.

'Awesome special effects,' said Mitchell. He looked around, as if he expected Miss Pythia to reappear through a secret door. She didn't.

'Miss Pythia's not coming back, is she?' I said.

Nathan shook his head.

'Nope,' said Daisy-May. 'These strange new teachers are just the same as the normal ones – they never stick around for long.'

'So you admit that Miss Pythia wasn't entirely normal, then?' I asked.

Nathan giggled and Daisy-May smiled. 'Let me see… There was the time travel, the weird premonitions, and her eventual evaporation. Not entirely normal I suppose, but not the strangest teacher we've ever had,' she said.

I glanced across the stage to where Miss Pythia had been standing just moments before.

'I wonder who we'll get next.'

As it turned out, we only had to wait until Monday morning to find out. We waited in the classroom while Ms Weebly fetched our new teacher from the school office.

We tried to guess who it would be.

'Miss Pythia said 5B so it must be someone with a B surname,' said Daisy-May.

AJ took a deep breath.

'BLACK, BOTTICELLI, BUGG, BROOMFIELD, BUTTER–'

There was a cough from the doorway.

'Bland,' said a voice, sounding out each letter of the word precisely.

A tall figure wearing a long coat stepped into the classroom, with Ms Weebly following behind.

'I am Dr Bland,' he said. 'Your new teacher.'

He didn't sound particularly pleased or displeased about this. We all stared at him.

Under his black coat, he wore grey trousers and a buttoned-up waistcoat. He had a stiff white collar that reached right up under his chin and a grey tie. His longish hair was wispy, grey and wavy. Even his skin had a grey tinge. He looked like a black and white photograph.

He stood before us blinking steadily and a funny feeling washed over me. A feeling that I'd seen him before. I put up my hand and Dr Bland nodded in my direction.

'Were you the one on the stage?' I asked, in a rush. 'The one in the mask? At *Play in a Day*? Was it you?' It was. I was sure of it.

Dr Bland raised an eyebrow at the question.

'No, that wasn't me.' His face barely moved

when he spoke. 'I have never met any of you before now.'

'IF YOU ARE A DOCTOR, WHY AREN'T YOU LOOKING AFTER ILL PEOPLE?' asked AJ.

Dr Bland pursed his lips.

'I am not that sort of doctor.' There was a sudden spark from his waistcoat pocket and his hand moved swiftly to tuck something back in. It looked like a jumble of wires.

Maybe Dr Bland was not quite as ordinary as he first appeared. Spotting teacher peculiarities was my speciality. I made a note.

Dr Bland stared at me and I put my pencil down.

'Now is probably a good time to tell you that I am not fond of children asking questions. You will learn a lot more from me if you keep your mouths firmly shut.'

He produced a thin cane from behind his back and swiped it in a crossways motion. It made a whistling noise as it cut through the air.

'Cool moves,' said Mitchell. We all giggled but Dr Bland stopped and brought the cane down on Mitchell's desk with a sharp THWACK!

'Silence!' he said.

There was silence. Ms Weebly smiled at Dr Bland approvingly and he put the cane down and straightened his tie.

'Now stop fidgeting, everyone, and sit with your backs straight. Our lesson is about to begin.'

5B TEACHERS

✳ <u>Dr Bland</u>: so it looks like we have another new teacher. Dr Bland might seem grey and boring but I've got a feeling that he's just as <u>mysterious</u> as the others. He looks as though he just stepped out of a history book. And I'm <u>sure</u> it was him on stage during the play. Then there are those wires in his pocket: what are they about? I'm looking forward to finding out!

The end...?

Keep an eye out for
Arlo's next adventure!

DISCUSSION POINTS

Arlo faces many challenges during the story, but he also has to deal with consequence.
- How do decisions and consequences vary from character to character?
- Are there other characters who struggle with the consequences of their actions?
- Why is consequence important in the story?

5P's play is a retelling of a very old myth.
- Why do we retell old myths in different ways?
- Can you think of any myths or fairy tales that have been retold?
- Are there any differences between the story Miss Pythia told and 5P's play? What did they keep the same?

5P learn something very important along the way: teamwork.
- How is teamwork explored in the book?
- Why do 5P have to work as a team for the play to succeed?
- What does working as a team teach us?